This present belongs to:

....

First published in Great Britain in 2017 by Hodder and Stoughton
This edition published in 2017

Copyright © Steve Antony 2017

Hodder Children's Books
An imprint of Hachette Children's Group
Part of Hodder and Stoughton
Carmelite House
50 Victoria Embankment
London EC4Y 0DZ

ISBN 978 1 444 92786 3
Printed in China

1 3 5 7 9 10 8 6 4 2

An Hachette UK Company
www.hachette.co.uk

Hodder
Children's
Books

MIX
Paper from
responsible sources
FSC® C104740

Thank You, Mr Panda

Steve Antony

Who are all
the presents
for, Mr Panda?

My friends.

This is for Mouse.

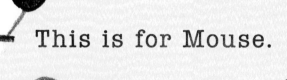

A present for
me, Mr Panda?

It's the thought
that counts.

But it's
too big.

A gift for me,
Mr Panda?

But I have eight legs.

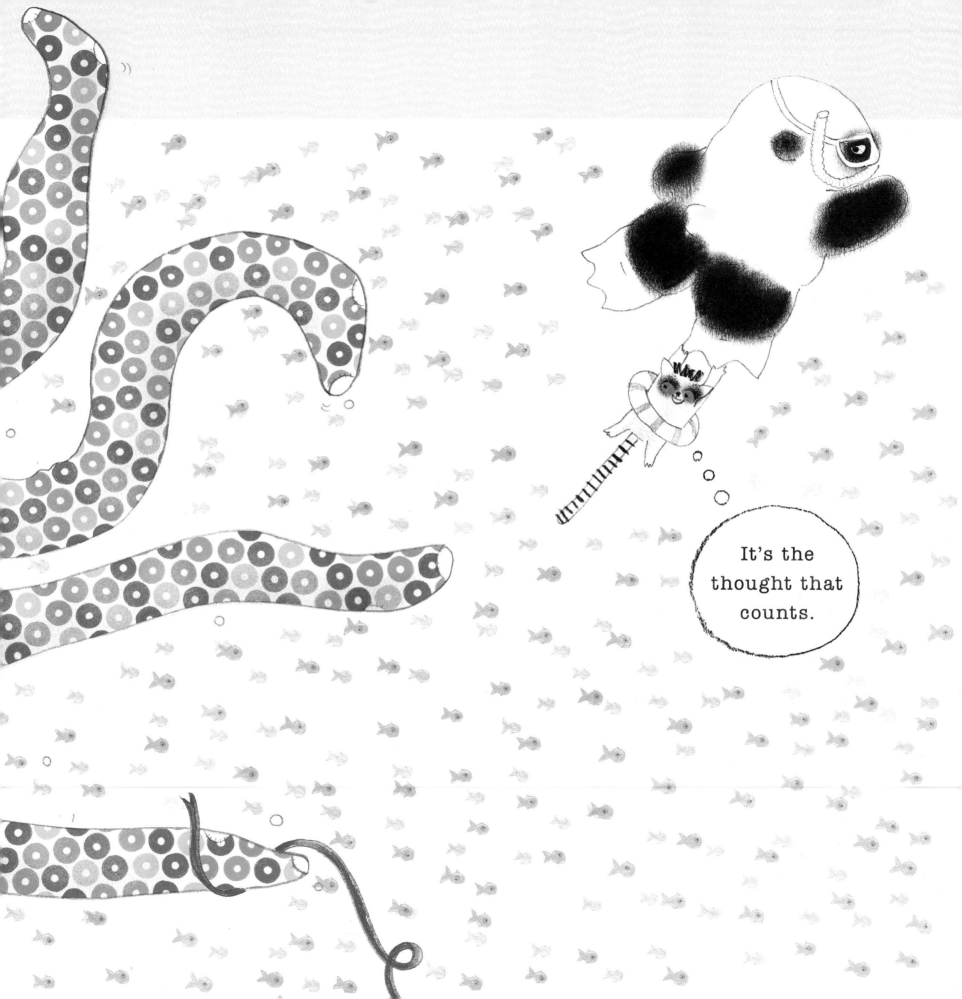

This is for Elephant.

I will open it later.

And this is for
Mountain Goat.

Something for me, Mr Panda?

But it's too heavy.

It's the thought that counts.

Who is the
last present
for, Mr Panda?

It's for you.

Thank you, Mr Panda!

You're welcome,
but remember...

...it's the thought that counts.